Tel Sono

Tel Sono

The Japanese Reformer

Tel Sono

Tel Sono
The Japanese Reformer

ISBN/EAN: 9783337075040

Printed in Europe, USA, Canada, Australia, Japan

Cover: Foto ©Raphael Reischuk / pixelio.de

More available books at **www.hansebooks.com**

THE JAPANESE REFORMER

AN AUTOBIOGRAPHY

NEW YORK
PRINTED BY HUNT & EATON
1890

INTRODUCTION.

To write the introduction to this autobiography is indeed a pleasure and privilege. Though not a year has passed since Miss Tel Sono and I first met, we have learned "to know each other's hearts," as she so sweetly expresses it, and to enter into each other's hopes.

God's hand in the history of nations is oftentimes traced; his hand in the history of a life is here as easily traced. The groping of a heathen mind after the true God through long, weary years, until the glad finding day, is here shown. The picture of a remarkable career crowded with worthy deeds, and yet but the shadow of one more sublime toward which it looks, is here drawn. And a purpose high, noble, and Christ-like is here found.

From the "Land of the Rising Sun" Tel Sono came to where the beams of the Sun of Righteousness could find their way into the misty darkness of her heart and dispel the gloom. With a woman's heart she felt for woman's woe, and came with a woman's fixedness of purpose, determined, at whatever cost, to alleviate that woe. Home and honor she left to dwell alone in a strange land and fill the

lowliest place, that thus she might the more effectu-
ally work for the accomplishment of that purpose.
Such a spirit God himself honored by coming in to
quicken, energize, and vivify.   And now, the eternal
Light filling all her soul, she will return to be a
mighty power in dispelling Japan's night, and making that fair country in very truth a land of the rising sun—the rising, triumphant, all-conquering Sun
of Righteousness.

All cannot share in what has made my life richer
and stronger—the friendship of this heroic, noble
woman and the inspiration of her simple, unfaltering
faith; but all can breathe something of the freshness
and vigor and spirit of her presence by the reading of
this story of her life.   HESTER ALWAY.

CONTENTS.

CHAPTER IX.

CHAPTER X.

' CHAPTER XI.

TEL SONO,

THE JAPANESE REFORMER.

CHAPTER I.

PARENTAGE — STUDIES — THOUGHTS OF GOD—"TESA."

My ancestors were of high descent, and very wealthy. Moan Waka Sono, my grandfather, who lived in Nagoya, was a philosopher. When over fifty years old he came to believe in a God in heaven, and built a room for prayer. There he always prayed looking toward heaven and ringing a bell which he held in his right hand. Sometimes he would sit down in the room and remain engaged in prayer for hours, not moving nor taking any nourishment.

He began to give all his wealth to the destitute, and soon became very poor; but he did not care about his poverty, and always said, " Human wealth is unprofitable. I cannot carry it away when I die."

His eldest daughter, my aunt, a very fine poetess, was fond of travel. Once when traveling alone, as was her custom, she was met in a mountain-pass by a thief. As a part of every woman's education in Japan is skill in combat, my aunt was ready to defend herself. When he made the attempt to rob her she adroitly pushed him down and held him while she reproved him for his evil deeds, explaining to him the right and wrong paths. "I will send you to judgment if you do not repent and stop this wicked business," she said. "I will go to right work now," he said. "I have been doing this work only a few months, but, after what you have said, can do it no longer." Then he wished her to spend the night with him. She accepted the invitation, received good care from himself and wife, and was brought on her journey the following day by them.

When grandfather became very old she took him to her home and nursed him. One snowy winter afternoon he lay down after dinner to rest, saying in verse, "He has kept my life for over eighty years. Now may I rest in happiness!" Soon he fell asleep, never to awaken.

He had four children, three sons and one daughter. The daughter, I have said, was a poetess, the first-born son the doctor of a prince, the second a teacher of war-tactics, and the youngest, my father, a philosopher and doctor. He first studied philosophy and traveled through the country. Once he sojourned in a place where the minister had a very fine old picture on which he had always wanted a poem written, but could find no person able to write it. My father wrote the desired poem, with which the people and minister were so pleased they wished him to stay a while and teach for them. They built him a house and gave him kind attention. He gathered many scholars about him and remained there three years. The people wanted him to marry and make his home among them. Accordingly, arrangements were made and he married the daughter of a village governor. Shortly after the marriage he took her to the home of his sister, leaving her there to study, as she was not an educated woman, while he went away to study medicine.

After he was graduated they went to the city of Tokio, where he began his practice of medicine. Many kings called him to serve them, but he loved freedom and would never go. His old scholars also called him to return to them. Shortly after my birth my parents returned to Ebalaki, where they remained.

I was the second eldest of four children. One brother was a doctor, and my sister was a teacher in a public school for women. This school was established by her, and was the first school for women in my native place.

My good father never worshiped idols, neither would he allow me to do so, but counseled me when a little girl to minister to the needs of the destitute whenever an opportunity presented itself, resting assured that a pure life and kind deeds would be rewarded. His advice I have never forgotten, and have ever tried to live in accord with it, gladly sharing whatever I had with those not so favored. Near my home lived a poor widow who loved me very much. One evening I saw that the back of her dress was badly torn, and I said, "O, *bayah*" (a word used in addressing middle-aged or old women of the lower class), "your dress is torn behind." "Yes, *ojosama*" (miss), she said, "will you give some clothes to bayah?" I said I would, and running home quickly I got a summer gown of my father's, a garment worn by both men and women, and gave it to her. The next morning she came to thank my mother for the garment. My mother looked first at one, then at the other, and for some little time could not speak for laughing; but finally she said it was all right.

Sometimes she scolded me for doing those things, but my father always said, "She is doing a good work. Do not be angry with her." Indeed, I gave my mother much trouble by my generosity, for when she had the dinner ready I many times would carry it out the back door and give it to the poor. My clothing also I frequently gave away. One winter afternoon—for we have our cold seasons in Japan— I took two little girls to a Buddhist garden. They were very scantily clothed and shivered in the cold north wind. My heart was moved with compassion, and, going with them behind the hedge, I took off two of my warm garments and gave one to each.

When thirteen years of age I began the study of Japanese poetry with my father. The poems made me think and wonder, while many questions arose in my mind. My father understood me better than any one else, and to him I went with my questions. "Father," I said, "who is the true God, and where is he?"

"I do not know, my child, but think he is somewhere in the sky."

"Who made the earth, the people, the animals, and all other things?" I questioned.

"It may be the works of God," he answered, "because human power is not sufficient."

From that time I always thought there was one true God who dwelt in the sky, though for my thoughts I had no other evidence than the feeling that there must be some power in the universe greater and higher than mere human power.

That same year an incident occurred that showed me very plainly the utter folly of idol-worship. While walking to school one morning with a friend, a girl several years older than myself, she told me about an altar which her father had erected to a very popular god. She said all her friends and neighbors came together every night to worship him, and asked me to meet them with my mother. In answer to my question regarding what kind of a god he was, she said his name was Otamasama, and that he was very mighty and strong; in fact, that he was the most high God. I said, "O no! he is an idol, and my mother and I will never worship idols." "I think he will kill you because you speak against him," she exclaimed loudly. "Very well," I said, " if he is the true God I hope he will kill me, because I have always searched for him and shall be glad to know him. However, I do not believe this idol can kill me." She said he certainly would kill me because I doubted his being God. " Will you promise me one thing?" I said. " You have asked your god to kill me, and if he does not do it will you apologize for your hatred and angry words?" She thought a little while, then said she would.

As we neared home I charged her not to forget her promise, for I could see by her anxious face that she was greatly troubled. In the evening my most intimate friend told me that Tesa was going to have a meeting at her house, and was going to ask her god to kill me that very night. I told her not to let that trouble her, for I was certain her god was only an idol, but that I would go over and see her pray to him. Then throwing my apron over my head I hurried to her home. I could not open the gate, so crawled through a hole in the hedge and crept up to the parlor window. In Japan the custom is to have the parlor open on the lawn at the rear of the house. Windows made of fine heavy paper reach to the ground. No curtains are used, and the outside shutters are not closed until bed-time. In this large room, or parlor, was erected the altar. I was partly screened from view by the surrounding trees and shrubbery, and, tearing a small hole in the paper window, witnessed unobserved the ceremonies carried on inside.

There were about fifty people kneeling around the altar, on which was placed a paper image. Some clasped their hands and looked up at the image; some bowed before it until their faces almost touched the floor, and some had tinsel balls strung together like a necklace which they rubbed between the palms of their hands, making a jingling sound, while all gave vent to exclamations of praise and adoration. Their faces were bathed in perspiration from their intense earnestness in calling for the spirit to come and enter that paper idol.

Before the altar stood a large iron pan in which a slow fire was kept burning, filling the room with smoke. I watched just as earnestly as they prayed, wondering what a spirit could be like. Then one of their number bowed very low directly in front of the altar and made a long prayer in which he besought the spirit to come and take possession of him.

After a long time he shook the image, causing the paper ribbons to make a rustling noise, an indication to the people that his prayer was not being answered. "I feel very strange to-night," he said. "Why does not the spirit come? I think there must be some unbelievers here." He looked over the company, but found only his members there; then he opened the window and saw me sitting behind a small evergreen tree at the corner under the window. "A little unbelieving girl has confused our prayers to-night!" he exclaimed. Tesa's father came out to where I was, and, on recognizing me, said to the prophet, "This little girl is the daughter of Dr. Tesai Sono. She and my daughter are school-mates." Then the prophet told him to drive me away quickly.

He wanted to do as he was bidden, so opened the gate and told me to go right home. "No," I said, "I will not go until your daughter acknowledges to me that her god is an idol. She promised me this morning that she would do that if he did not kill me to-night." Her father called to her and told her to come out, but she refused because she was afraid.

Her mother came and begged me to obey her and go home, saying she would make acknowledgment in her daughter's stead and would give me fruit and cake besides. That satisfied me, for I felt that I had come off victorious.

I said, "I will excuse her for your sake." It was then about ten o'clock, and I ran home with my apron full of cake and fruit, but said nothing to my parents about where I had been.

CHAPTER II.

FATHER'S SICKNESS—A PRAYER.

WHEN I was fourteen years old my father fell sick, and the doctors said that he could not live more than two or three days. This made my mother, sister, and brothers so sad that I could not stay with them in the house. I determined to pray to the true God for my father's life, so, taking my best friend, Otama, with me into a secluded place in the garden near a well, I told her what I intended to do, and asked her to help me.

She listened earnestly while I talked, peering into my face too astonished to make any reply. At last she said, " Are you crazy to-night?" " No, I am not crazy. My mother, sister, and brothers are very sorrowful and my own heart is almost broken; therefore I have decided to offer my own life as a sacrifice for my father's."

At this point she threw her arms around me, and after we had wept for some time in each other's embrace she said, " I will do as you wish, but if you die I want to die with you."

The ceremonies connected with prayer for the life of a friend were very solemn and awful, involving the sacrifice of the suppliant's life for that of the sick person, if necessary. First the hair was cut off and

offered as a sacrifice—the most precious which could
be offered; then the body was stripped, and cold
water poured over it to purify and make prayer
acceptable.

Taking a razor, I cut off my hair close to the scalp
and hung it up under a tree. Next I took off all my
clothing, and, throwing it down on the grass, seated
myself on a board by the well. Otama then poured
three buckets full of water on my head, causing it to
run down over my entire body. I shook so with the
cold, both from the water and the north wind that was
blowing, that I could not utter one word of prayer at
first; but after a while I did not feel the cold quite
so much, and looking up toward the sky began to pray
thus: " O, true God! If you stay somewhere in the
sky, please hear my voice! Please let me die for my
father, for if he dies my mother will die also. Save
the lives of my father and mother, I pray, O God,
and I will sacrifice to you not only my hair, but my
soul and body. If you do not spare my father's
life I hope you will kill me just now! O, is there
no true God in the world? I am so hungry to
hear God's voice! O, please speak to me and
save my father's life ? "

After Otama had poured the water on my head
she sat down on the grass behind me and listened to
my prayer. Just as I was uttering the last sentence
she cried with aloud voice. This attracted my grandmother's attention, and, taking a lighted candle in

her hand, she with my nurse hurried into the garden. When they discovered us they were greatly shocked at my condition. My nurse caught up my clothing and wrapping it around my naked body carried me to the house and put me down by the fire, while my grandmother and friend followed us.

Grandmother looked into my face, put her hand on my head, and whispered something to my nurse; then both cried for a long time.

It was about eleven o'clock when nurse took me to bed, my friend staying to sleep with me. Not being able to sleep, I got up about midnight and went softly through the hall to my father's sick-room. Listening carefully at the door, I heard some one laugh. "That is my mother's voice," I said. "I believe God has heard my prayer and made my father better, or mother would not be laughing." Just then mother came out and saw me standing by the door. She looked into my face and said, "My dear, father is a little better; you did him good. Now run right to bed and get a good sleep; then you may get up early and come to see him."

I obeyed, and slept soundly all the rest of the night. Rising early, I went to my father's room and looked anxiously into his face to see how he was. "My dear," he said, speaking slowly and in a very weak voice, "I am much better this morning, and think I will soon be well; you need not feel troubled about

2

me any more.   I hope that you will go to school to-day
and have good lessons."

I ran away by myself and cried for joy. " Surely
there is a true God somewhere," I said, and prayed
again : " O, true God, I thank you very much for sav-
ing my father's life.   Now I wish you would please
keep him alive many years, and take my life any time
instead."   Then I went to school and played with the
children.

My mind was perfectly at rest about my father
from that time, and by Christmas, two months later,
he was entirely well.

CHAPTER III.

MARRIAGE—A REBELLION—RETURN TO FATHER'S HOUSE.

At the age of nineteen my parents betrothed me to an officer of the king's treasure, to whom I was soon married. He took me to his home, where his parents and two sisters-in-law also lived. The following year (1866) there arose a rebellion that caused much excitement for a time but was soon quelled. I had been spending the night with my mother, and very early in the morning we were awakened by the firing of guns in rapid succession. Mother's maid came running into the room and told us to get up at once, that the rebels were fighting in our town, Manaba. Rising quickly, I looked toward my husband's home and saw that it was completely enveloped in smoke and fire. "I must go right home!" I exclaimed. Mother remonstrated with me, and said, "You cannot go, child, for you might have to pass right through the blazing fire and be burned to death."

But I scarcely knew what she was saying; and, dressing hurriedly, I hastened home. My husband and father-in-law being officers of the king's court were of course on duty, and I found my mother and sisters-in-law with their treasures tied up and just ready to escape from the house. "Mother, I think

you had better wait a while," I said, "because when
father wants more arms he will send a messenger for
them, and if we leave who will give them to him?
Our goods will be stolen if we leave the house; besides, the fighting will probably stop soon, and if it
does not the king will have us taken to his fort."
But my mother-in-law said she could not wait so long
for deliverance, and that she was going to look after
her own life and the lives of her daughters. "If you
want to stay alone and watch the house you may
do so," she said.

After they had gone I washed my face, changed
my dress, took one of my husband's swords, and
seated myself on the front door step to watch the
battle.

The enemies were soon scattered, and by evening
our town was in peace and quiet. When peace was
restored those who had fled from their homes in fear
crept quietly back like so many spiders, carrying their
bundles with them.

My husband was called to Tokio on matters of
business occasioned by the rebellion, and was detained
there a year. On his return I noticed that he had
begun to drink wine. Many times I begged him to
stop, but he would not listen to me. In my country
the *Enarimasure*, or Fox holiday, is celebrated the
second day of February. Small temples are built in the
yard of each king, and sumptuous feasts are spread for
the officers and their guests. On one such occasion my

husband spent all day feasting and playing with his friends, and came home at seven o'clock in the evening very drunk and wanted me to drink wine with him. "No," I said, "I will *never* give you wine to drink in my house." He left the room, but soon came back bringing a bottle of wine, and commanded me to make a wine feast for him. This I refused to do, and took the glass from his hand, out of which he was about to drink. At this he became very angry and struck me. Then I concluded that it would be better for me to go back to my father's house, and to do so at once, while my husband was rich. Should I wait until he became poor he would say that I left him because of his poverty and would hate me. Accordingly, I took my little daughter, then three years old, and returned to my home, May 2, 1871. My grandmother had died the year before, and in her house, which was in the same yard with my father's, I lived with one servant. There I established a free school for the poor and taught it for three years.

My father and I resumed our study together, and in addition to other studies we read books of law.

My daughter's future, and how to provide for it, was a great question in my mind. She must be educated, and I wondered what I, a woman, could do to earn money sufficient. At last I decided to be a lawyer. Closing my school, and leaving my daughter with my mother, I went to Tokio to pursue my studies.

CHAPTER IV.

PRACTICING LAW—DISASTROUS FIRES—FATHER'S DEATH.

FOR three months I held the position of secretary of judgment, and then began the practice of law.

There is in my country no tradition of a woman lawyer, and up to the present time I have been the only one.

Many people came to see me every day as I went to court, and when I passed through the yard the people on both sides of the judicial and assize courts would stand up to gaze at me. They thought it very wonderful and strange for a woman to be a lawyer.

That year much that was new from America and other countries was introduced into Japan, among which was the telegraph, steam-carriages, electric light, and photography.

At this time two poets who lived in the city of Tokio, N. Ohash and S. Keta, wrote one hundred poems about the wonderful things Japan now possessed. One poem was about the woman lawyer, and thus, when the book, *Tokishensh*, was published, my name became known throughout Japan.

For twelve years I followed the practice of law, and my career was recognized by all as most successful. In this profession the low position of woman was brought more clearly than ever before my mind, and in my heart there burned a desire to elevate her by giving her an education.

My wisest course to accomplish this object seemed to be to visit America and learn the customs of a people where woman stood on a level with man. But no opportunity for me to leave my business presented itself. One day a poor woman who had been ensnared by a wicked man, and led to make a great mistake through her ignorance, was tried and condemned.

How my heart burned! I grew impatient of delay. Soon I would be too old to do the work now within my power. To America I must go, and that at once. Four days after the decision against the poor ignorant woman, and my decision following that, I set sail for America. But before describing my life in America I will relate a few incidents descriptive of my benevolent work during the twelve years in Tokio.

As the buildings in my country are mostly of wood, fires often break out, and, sweeping along with terrible force, destroy whole blocks. Such a fire raged through the streets of the poor one winter night, the loud ringing of fire-bells awakening me about eleven o'clock. The river which ran through the street was frozen over so that water enough to put out the flames could not be obtained, and when morning dawned the homes of almost three hundred poor families had been burned to the ground. At an early hour I opened a store to feed these homeless ones. To each person I gave fifteen pounds of rice, and to the children candy and crackers. For two weeks I carried on this benevolent work, and about three months after received a letter from the emperor in acknowledgment of my work.

At another time a fire broke out about a mile from my house and quite near many buildings which I was just having put up. The night was calm at first, but suddenly a strong west wind rose, driving the flames with fierce rapidity until my new buildings were reached and then my home. Thirty-six strong men came to the rescue, carrying out all my household goods, but being quite unable to save the buildings. All the night they guarded my goods, while I went to a quiet place to rest. The following morning I took them with me to a great restaurant, gave them a good dinner, and offered money to each. The money they would not accept, saying it was their duty to help in time of fire. "We have often helped others," they said, "but never had such a feast after our work, and we certainly never saw any one with such a pleasant face after being burned out. You have ever been ready to help us, and we are glad to do this for you." Then one of them told about my gardener, who it seemed would not leave my home to save his own, saying if his was destroyed he could bring his family and live with me. I told them that I understood all their kindness and appreciated it, but could not rest without paying them for their services, and that the very experience through which I had just passed would enable me to make more money in my business. At this they gladly received the money. Then they took me back to my home, and standing in rank before the door sang a happy song.

Through the kindness of friends a new home was quickly built for me. My loss through this fire was very great.

The third year of my business life my father came to visit me. " I have come to bid you good-bye," he said, " for I have a sickness with which I must soon die."

He brought a letter from my mother in which she charged me to comfort him and give him good care, for he would probably die that year. After three months he returned home, and soon becam every sick. When I went home to nurse him he said, " You must not trouble. The end of my life is come, and such is the will of heaven." He had been accustomed to say, when he saw wicked persons come into danger and distress, " It is the judgment of Heaven."

A month later, on the evening of October 3, 1876, he told us, " I shall die about four o'clock in the morning." Then he dictated a short poem, which my sister wrote:

" He in whose hand my breath has been held now opens his hand,
And my soul goes away."

At the hour named he passed away.

CHAPTER V.

As in childhood I had loved to help the needy, so in womanhood, with increased opportunities, this work was one of my chief delights.

Every year on Christmas eve I invited to my home the women and men who worked for me. To each one I lent money that they might prepare for the New-year and canceled the old year's debt, telling them they must work well the next year. On the New-year, January 7, I invited all the poor in the neighborhood, with my working-people, to a soup dinner.

Each at my request brought a handful of something to put in the soup, which was being prepared in a large iron kettle. They all gathered around me when it was done, while I tasted to find how good the soup was and who had brought in the best thing for it, giving credit to each one for good taste. When the dinner had been eaten I gave parcels of clothing, comforters, towels, stockings, aprons, cakes, candies, and other things to the poor, and to my rich friends who came to see the condition of the poor I gave boxes tied with bright ribbons, which they were not to open until they went home. In these boxes were baked potatoes, turnips, and onions. Early the next morning the poor would return to thank me, and my friends to laugh over the funny contents of their boxes. I remember now with pleasure these New-year days and the glad faces of my people on such occasions.

One morning not long after the New-year my hand-maid came to my sitting-room to tell me the gardener was crying in the back kitchen. I bade her call him in, and inquired concerning his trouble. He said his mother had died the night before, and that he had no money to bury her. "I cannot ask you for money," he said, "for you are always doing so much for us." However, I gave him the needed money for the funeral expenses. To the poor sick I used to send my doctor, also money and food, and many times paid their funeral expenses.

In December, 1879, a young man came to me with the following sad story : "Two weeks ago a gentle-man came to the clothing store where I worked and said that his family wanted some clothes for the New-year. He chose high-priced goods, and at his request I carried them to the house that his family might see them. Then he asked me to leave them all night until his mother came home, as they wanted to ask her opinion about what was best to buy. After some consideration I decided to leave them, as the home was not a poor one, and I thought he probably was an

officer of the law. But I could not sleep that night,
because in leaving the goods I had broken the law of
the store and I felt I had done wrong. Early next
morning I went to the house, but it was shut up and
no person answered my knock. My heart beat like
dashing waves or the quick ringing of bells. All day
I watched, and in the evening saw the family return.
I went to the man and asked him for the goods. He
said a person whom he owed had taken them away in
payment of his debt. He was sorry, he said, but the
only thing he could do was to give me three dollars
every month until the price was paid. After that he
would have nothing more to say to me. My master
has said that I must pay for the goods if I do not
bring them back to the store. He will not forgive
me, because he says others would do the same by and
by. I have no money to pay and am a stranger, having come from the far north country. Will you not
speak for me and get back the goods that I may return to my work?"

I felt very sorry for him, and went as he requested
to the man who had stolen the goods. The cause of
his committing the evil deed was easily explained.
He had been rich; then, on account of poor eye-
sight, his business had failed, but being proud he
wished to keep up a good appearance. I told him
judgment would come upon him for his wickedness,
his deceit, and theft. He was greatly ashamed and
afraid, knowing what I had said was true. When

I had finished talking he bowed down until his face almost touched the floor, saying, with tears : " Will you not save us with your great virtue ? I committed this iniquity because we have become poor on account of my failing eye-sight. " If you make this public I shall be sent to prison as you have said, and my dear mother, wife, and child will die with hunger. Please save my family."

His wife, who sat beside him, cried so loudly that his mother's attention was arrested, and she came down-stairs. His daughter also came in, and, though she did not know what was the trouble, stood by her father weeping. He said to her : " Dear, your father has committed a great sin, and this lady can send him to prison. What will you do if I go to prison? You will die of hunger, and so will your mother and grandmother. Ask this lady to forgive my sin for the sake of our family." Then the child, who was about ten years old, and the grandmother of seventy and the wife, all came to my side and worshiped me, their tears falling like rain. I felt most sorry for the grandmother and child, who had not known of the wrong that had been done, especially for the poor grandmother. Her face was thin, her hair white, and she looked ready to die. My heart began to move with compassion for them. I asked the man what restitution he could make. He said he received thirty dollars from the emperor every month, and could pay ten out of that money until the eighty for which he had sold the goods was refunded. Taking him with me, I went to the man who bought the goods and told him the circumstances. He was greatly troubled about having stolen property, and on my paying him eighty dollars collected the goods and sent them home with me. I put them into the hands of the young man, who, with a grateful heart, took them back to the store. I accompanied him and excused him to his master, who allowed him to come back to his work. The debtor promised to pay me ten dollars every month, and thus the matter was settled.

Three years later I read in a newspaper the sad condition of a poor woman, who lived in a wretched street with a blind, sick husband and two children, one a baby. The paper said the children were crying of hunger, all were like skeletons, and the mother was almost crazy with grief. I at once went to see if what I had read was true, taking some food in my buggy to give them if they were in need. I reached the place only to find their condition worse than had been described. The man was lying on the floor covered with a thin comforter, and the children on a large piece of thick paper covered with an old sheet. They were dressed in summer clothes, the bones stood out on their faces, and they were in such a weak condition they could not move. The first thing I did was to give them the food which I had brought. The woman acted very strangely from the first; her face turned red when she saw me, and she did not seem to receive very willingly what I gave her. She said to her husband, " Miss Tel Sono has called, and she has brought many things for us; she has also given me much money." " Who did you say had visited us?" he said, starting up. " What shall I do? Please cover my face." Then he assumed a worshipful attitude toward me, as did also his wife, their tears falling fast. A long while I stood in the kitchen wondering who they were. At last I remembered this was the man who had stolen the goods, and I then understood their strange manner. He had not kept his promise in regard to paying me, but after sending twenty dollars had moved away, and I had heard nothing from him.

I told them not to trouble about that, the matter had quite passed from my mind, and that I then forgave them. " You are in trouble now," I said, " therefore I will think of you as my new friends, and do what I can to help you."

I sent them warm clothes, and my doctor attended the sick man. A month later he died, and was buried at my expense. Seven days after the funeral I sent the family to their relatives in the north.

As I look back now I understand that it was God who visited this man in judgment for his sin. I forgave him, but he could not escape the justice of God.

Very early one October morning a poor woman

came to see me. My maid told her she had better
come later, as her mistress had not yet risen. She
would not move from the front step, however, but
pleaded that she might see me, saying I could save her
life. When the maid told me what the woman said
I had her called in. She was about forty years of
age, and wore a summer dress though the day was
cold. In answer to my questions, she told me the following story : " Four months ago my husband and I
came from the south country to the city of Tokio that
he might be convenient to his business. We brought
our clothes and other personal belongings, but sold
our house and household furniture, and since being
here have boarded.

" At first my husband returned from business every
day, then he did not come home so often. Three
weeks ago he returned and said: ' My business has
failed and my money is all lost. I need money to-
night to begin business again. Will you lend me
your possessions ? I will give them back to you in a
week with a reward.' I did as he asked, giving him
both my money and valuables. Every day since I
have looked for him, but in vain.

" Soon after his disappearance I began to receive
letters from those whom he owed, and creditors began
to call on me. This was the first that I knew of his
having contracted a large debt, and the knowledge
occasioned me much sadness. I searched in his business places for some trace of him but could find none.

A week ago my landlord said he could not keep me any longer unless I paid my board. On my promising to give him some money soon he allowed me to stay a little while longer.

" I determined to seek help from a rich aunt whom I had not visited for ten years on account of having angered her by a mistake I made, hoping she would forgive the past. When I told her of my trouble and asked her to lend me some money she coldly said she could lend me no money unless I mortgaged something. I had nothing to mortgage except the clothing I wore, but my need was great; so taking off some of my garments I gave them to her in exchange for a small sum of money.

" With this I paid my board, then searched again for my husband. This morning the landlord said he could keep me no longer. 'I feel very sorry for you,' he said, 'for I do not believe that you will find your husband.' Then he told me of you, whom he knew to be a kind, brave woman, and said he believed you would help me. That is why I am come to you."

While considering her case the words of a wise man came to my mind: " If a bird escape from one hunter's hand and seek refuge in the hand of another hunter, the latter would not take her life." Then I decided that as the poor woman had come to me for help I could not turn her away. " You may come and live with me," I said, " and I will help you." At this she wept for joy. Taking her with me, I went

3

to her landlord, paid the remainder of her debt for
board, and had her bring what few things she owned
to my home.   Then I went and spoke to her aunt
about the wrong she had done in taking the clothes
her niece was wearing. She was greatly ashamed,
and gave back the clothes, but would not keep her
niece, saying I was free to do for her as I wished.

For a year and a half I kept the woman in my
home, to the great anxiety of my friends, who feared
she would rob me. I told them they need not trouble;
she was only a poor woman, and not able to carry
away my goods. When I gave her any thing the
same as my family had, she would begin to weep.
This I thought very strange, but was made to understand it when I too became a stranger in a strange
land.   Often the kind words spoken to me when
lonely and sad have received no other answer than a
flood of tears.

CHAPTER VI.

ARRIVAL IN AMERICA—FIRST EXPERIENCES.

IT was the 19th day of December, 1885, that I set sail for America, arriving in San Francisco the 7th of January, 1886.

Before leaving my country I wrote the following poem:

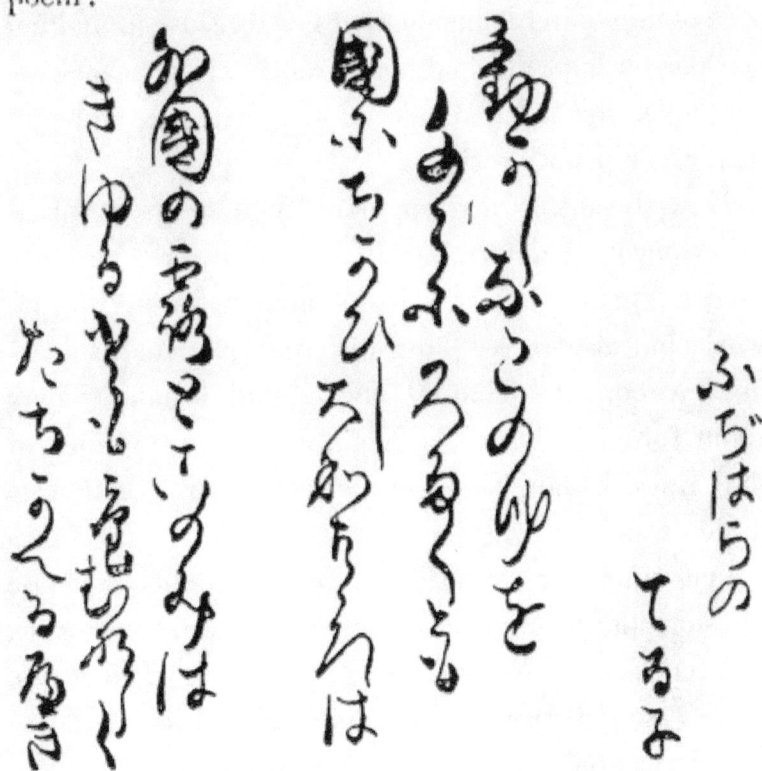

"My dear native land, my heart will never change its purpose, my duty to you will never be forgotten.

If my purpose cannot be perfected I will never return to you, but will die in the strange country, and there my body will turn to dust."

To all who had hired money of me I gave back the notes which I held against them, valued at over one thousand dollars.

Three months after my arrival in San Francisco the Bank of Japan, in which my money was deposited, failed. When I heard of that I concluded it would not have been right for me to use this money, which had been obtained in the business of law, because in making one person happy I had made another sad, in making one love me I had made another hate me, and that surely could not be right.

Now, I said, is my opportunity to gain a varied experience. I determined to do housework, not only to earn my living and make money for my future work, but also to see how different people lived. I hired a room in a colored family, and began to look about for employment. Not knowing any thing of the English language, my situation was rather a difficult and painful one.

One morning a gentleman came to the Japanese Mission and wanted a boy or girl to do house-work and cooking. No one was willing to go because it was so far from San Francisco and on a farm, but I wanted to see how American farmers lived and said I would go. He asked me if I could cook and do housework. As I could not speak English a friend answered for me and said I could do any work.

Then he engaged me, and we took the train to his home. His wife was waiting for us at the station with the buggy.

The family numbered six, the gentleman and his wife, their daughter, two hired men, and myself. The house was large, containing fourteen rooms, surrounded by a beautiful yard, in which were many flowers. The gentleman was a Mexican, and his wife a very proud German woman. She was angry because I could not speak English, and knew so little about housework, as it gave her trouble to teach me; and she would scold her husband for engaging me. Every morning, to atone for his mistake, he would get up early and teach me how to cook the breakfast. His wife taught me at dinner-time, and in about ten days I could do the work. One morning I made the biscuits without any baking-powder, so the next time she had her daughter make them for me to bake; but I did not know how long to let them stay in the oven. At dinner-time, after ringing the first bell, I looked at them and saw they were all black. I felt so ashamed and troubled that I hid them under the wood in the kindling box. She called me to bring in the biscuits, but I could not; so she came into the kitchen, and, not finding them, asked me where they were. I said, " Please excuse me! Please excuse me." I was very much afraid, because when angry she would slap her

daughter, so I ran and hid in the closet. A long time
after I told her about it and she laughed very much,
as she had then learned to love me.

I had to work very hard from morning until night,
and, as I had no time to study, decided to hide every
day for twenty minutes and read my books. Often I
studied until twelve o'clock at night, and in that way
succeeded in translating the Third and Fourth Readers.
Not being accustomed to work, it caused my hands to
become sore and my limbs to swell so that I had to
lie down to study at night. When my friends saw
the books I translated they were surprised and very
much pleased.

I asked Mr. Meyama, my pastor, to find me a room
for which I would have to pay but little or nothing.
He answered laughingly that he could not unless I
were willing to stay down cellar in the darkness. I
said I would try it, so he went with me to see a room
under the Chinese Mission. It had no windows, but a
little light came from a hole through which I could see
the feet of the people as they passed by on the street.
As I had no money to pay rent I decided to stay there.

Mr. Meyama swept and washed the floor, then
brought a candle and lamp, an old bedstead, and a
sheet from the mission. He told me to sew the sheet
up, leaving one end open. When I had done so he
took it away, and after a while returned carrying
what I thought was a large white post. He put it on
the bedstead and said it was my bed. "Am I to

sleep on a big post?" I asked. It would become very comfortable, he said, after I had slept on it a week. When he had gone away I examined my strange-looking bed and found it was made of many white sticks. I did not believe I could sleep on it, and, going to Mr. Meyama, told him I thought he had played a joke on me. He said, "O no, indeed! That is truly a bed, a chip bed, as we call it in this country."

To convince me he showed me the young men's beds in the mission, and said they were just like mine at first. I returned to my cellar still greatly troubled at the thought of sleeping on such a queer thing. I went to school that night as usual, but on my return could not study for wondering where I should sleep. I tried to make the bed smooth and even by knocking it with my hands, but my attempts were vain. Then I tried another experiment, which seemed more successful, and went to bed only to fall out while asleep. This frightened me; but I determined to try it once again, and, taking the ropes from my trunk. tied the bed to the bedstead, and lay down this time to sleep till morning. During the days that followed I was very homesick, and every night dreamed of my native land. When I had time I would go to the top of a hill, and, sitting down on the grass, look out over the sea toward my home and say:

> " Ah, poor dismal heart!
> In a strange land art thou,
> Alone and friendless !

Thou hast no one to comfort thee,
No one to listen to the tale of thy woe,
The great deep lies between thee and home,
The clouds hang, a veil before thine eyes;
And in vain thou cryest
For native land and mother!"

I was indeed sad! The light of God's truth had not yet shone into my heart, my present position was very low, and the future was full of darkness in respect to the accomplishment of my work.

A Christian lady, Mrs. E. P. Keeney, who lived in the city of San Francisco, hearing of my wretched condition, took me to her home and showed me great kindness.

She taught me so that in three months I could read through the First and Second Readers. Then she went away and I returned to the cellar. During the day I worked at different places and at night attended school. On account of the dampness of the cellar I could not sit with my feet on the floor, so always sat on the bed to study, my little candle burning beside me. The bed, by the way, had become very comfortable, so that I used to say when coming in tired, "Dear bed, I love you better than the one at home!"

One midnight I was awakened by a great noise. Some colored men were quarreling and fighting. I was greatly afraid, for I thought that they might come into my room, because they had already kicked to pieces two doors in the next room. I felt very lonely and prayed, " O, true God, come and save me! I am very much afraid of that noise. Help, I pray, lest they come and kill me ! "

I believed God would make peace between them for me, and at once I ceased to fear. From that time I began to pray again to the " true God." I attended every meeting at the Japanese Mission, and tried to find him, but could not. Still I continued to pray alone in my cellar, and always felt happy after prayer.

CHAPTER VII.

SHORTLY after the incident before mentioned I left the cellar to work for a kind Christian lady, but in six weeks she was called to Ohio. Then Mrs. K. Waterman, a lady living near, said she would send me to school if I would come to her and wait on her daughter. She made this kind offer because she was in sympathy with my plans. Thus through her my way to gain an English education was opened.

For three days I attended the public school, and each day was questioned by the principal regarding my native country, my name, and age. "Are you sixteen or seventeen years old?" he said. For a long while I stood without making any reply, fearing to say that I was almost forty years old, lest he would not allow me to come to school.

He did not know what was going on in my heart, and explained again in very plain words his question. I could no longer be silent, so I said, "I am twenty-four years old." He looked surprised. "What? twenty-four years old! Are you sure?" That night Mrs. Waterman received a letter saying I could not attend the school.   I wept bitterly over the letter, refusing to leave my room or eat, so completely discouraged was I ; but Mrs. Waterman soon comforted me by saying she would send me to her daughter's school, which she immediately did.   In June, 1888, Mrs. Waterman's daughter died, and thus I had no work to do.   Though she did not say for me to go away, I decided to seek employment and a home elsewhere.   This time I went to work for a music-teacher. The family was very late in rising, thus keeping me late with my work.   In order to reach school in time I would have to run to catch the train ; but the conductor was kind, and used to wait when he saw me coming.

Wishing to know how to make American dresses I next went to live with a dress-maker.   One afternoon, while there, I was mending stockings in the sitting-room when some ladies came in.   They asked me why I was darning so many stockings.   "Because I wear out a pair almost every day," I said.   Then they wanted to know what number shoes I wore. I said I did not know, but that Japanese women's feet were very large.   Two of the ladies took off their shoes and tried them on my feet and found them quite large enough.   "You should wear shoes No. 4½ instead of No. 7," they said, laughing ; "then your stockings would not wear out so quickly."   After they had gone I went out and bought a pair of boots the proper size.   I laughed very heartily after when

I thought of how funny No. 7 shoes must have looked with the short skirts I then wore. I had not thought of my shoes being too large. I had only known that with every step they slipped up and down and that my feet felt very heavy. So anxious was I to study that my appearance received but little thought.

One afternoon, while waiting for the train to go over to the school, I went into a fruit-store to buy some bananas. As I was going out some one called after me, " You want cracker? You want cracker?" I thought it was the store-keeper, and said, " No, thank you." Twice again the question was asked. I answered in a little louder tone, for I did not like to be asked so often, " O no; I do not want any!" Then I noticed that those about me were laughing, and I looked around to find a parrot had been talking to me. I felt so ashamed that I hurried home without waiting for the train.

At this time my kind teacher, Mrs. Reid, said to me, " I have been thinking about you, and how very hard it is for you to meet the school expenses and your car-fare over here. If you are willing to teach drawing to the kindergarten children one hour every day you need not pay any thing for instruction."

This kind offer I gladly accepted.

CHAPTER VIII.

A TRYING PLACE.

I once went to an employment-office in San Francisco in search of work. The woman in charge said that she had a very hard place, where the lady could not keep a girl one week. I said I would like to try it. There were five children in the family, the father and mother, and an up-stairs girl.

One of my first orders was that I must not use over three shovels of coal at once, and that whenever I had any time I must chop coal and wood. Every night the lady gave me three cupfuls of oatmeal for breakfast, and that was all the breakfast they had. Very often I had not enough hot water because of not being allowed to keep much fire. She would come in very often to look at the stove and to see if I had used much coal; and the dampers were kept tied with wire so that they could not be opened to make the fire burn brightly. She and her husband drank coffee in the morning, but we were not allowed any; and if we wished tea she would put about ten or twelve leaves in our cups.

From five o'clock in the morning to ten o'clock at night I worked hard. For the up-stairs girl, who was about eighteen years old, I felt very sorry, because

she had not enough to eat. As she took care of the
children she had her meals with the family, and was
too much afraid of her mistress to eat much. She
asked me to give her a piece of bread every evening.
My only opportunity to get it was when taking off the
dishes, as the lady kept the keys of the pantry. So I
would slip a piece into my pocket and afterward put
it under the girl's pillow. She was very grateful for
the bread, and said she could not stay long if I went
away, because she had not strength to work so hard
without more food.

One morning after I had baked as usual I left the
bread and fresh biscuits on the table and went to my
ironing in the washing-room. Soon the lady called
me, and with an angry face said, " Did you eat five of
those biscuits?" I said I had not been in the
kitchen since having baked them. Then she called
the up-stairs girl and asked her, but she said she knew
nothing of them. And then she collected all the children before the table, the oldest one being eighteen
years of age, and examined each one. They all said
they had not taken the biscuits, though I thought they
very likely had eaten them, because they were always
hungry. Then she said she believed the milkman had
stolen them when he brought the milk into the
kitchen. The next time baking was done she commanded that the bread be left upon the same table, and
that I watch from some hiding-place when the milkman came in. "Wait until he gets out of the

kitchen," she said, "then call after him to 'give back those biscuits.' If he refuses, examine his pockets." Later she came in and wanted to know how he stole the biscuits and whether he gave them back or not; but I told her he did not take them and that he said he never stole her biscuits.

One Saturday I swept four bedrooms and put the children's large play-room in order between doing the cooking; but she said I did not do enough work for the money I received. I said, "Very well, you may get some one else to do your work. I cannot work any more than I am doing." About ten o'clock at night, a few days later, she said for me to begin ironing because the next day would be very busy. "No," I said, "I cannot work after ten o'clock." "You must obey me," she exclaimed. "If you wish I will go away at once, but I cannot obey such an unjust command." "If you do go away now I will not pay you for your past work." "Very well, I will never sacrifice my health for money. However, I will make public your conduct for the benefit of others." I began to pack my things to go away at once, but her husband asked me to stay two days and promised he would pay me honestly. The children also begged me to stay and excuse their mother.

The last morning I rose early, did all the morning work, and baked so that there would be enough bread to eat for a week after I had gone. "Why did you bake bread?" the lady said, coming into the kitchen.

"I do not want it, and you must pay me for it." I said I was very sorry, but would pay her seventy cents for the seven loaves. "You must pay one dollar for the time you spent," she said. I did so, and then I said, "I hope you will go to church now and get your heart in a better condition." A boy came from the Japanese Mission to help me carry my things. He looked on surprised when he saw me tying up the bread, and the lady watched my movements very closely. "You need not trouble about the bread," I said, "because it is mine." "Where are you going to take it?" she questioned. "To my pastor and friends. And now I want to thank you very much for the experience I have had with you. It has been good for me."

On my way to the mission I bought some tea and a half-roll of butter. After I made the tea we sat down to enjoy the bread. "You must eat with a relish," I said, "for this is very dear bread." Then I told them all about what had happened, and we had a merry time together.

CHAPTER IX.

CLEAR SHINING OF THE TRUTH—BAPTISM—ORGANIZING
OF A BENEVOLENT SOCIETY—WORK AMONG THE FALLEN.

As I went into these different homes, sixteen in
all, I went with the purpose to learn all possible. One
thing could not fail to impress me, and that was the
difference between those homes where God was honored and where he was not.

After many talks with my pastor and kind Christian ladies, and after studying the Bible diligently, I
came to know Christ as my Saviour. God spoke to
me, and I knew him to be the true God for whom I
had searched so many years. I was very happy, and
wanted to be baptized soon, and yet I wanted to do
something for my Saviour before I was baptized. It
was just at this time that my mother died in Japan,
her last words being, "My work is not perfected, for
I am only sixty years old ; but I must die."

One Saturday night at the meeting my pastor said,
" I wish all the brothers and sisters would, in Christ's
name, collect money for the new mission. It is very
near Christmas, and we want a new carpet for it."
He gave us some cards on which to write the names
of those who would subscribe. I took three, and at
once began to collect money from my friends, going

4

without my luncheon that I might spend the hour
that was free from lessons in collecting.

From thirty-three ladies I obtained money, and the
next Saturday gave it to Mr. Harris, who was much
pleased with what he called my "gift to God."

Then at the fair held for the purpose of paying off
the mission's building debt I took a table of Japanese
oranges and candy, making over fifty dollars in two
evenings and one day.

On Christmas day, 1889, I was baptized and joined
the Japanese Mission, with the fixed purpose to devote
my life to God's service.

After studying three years in the private school I
was graduated, 1889, and returned to San Francisco
to do hard work again that I might earn money
enough to attend some training-school for Christian
workers.

On my return the sad and destitute condition of
many of my country sisters appealed to my heart. I
determined to help them in some way, and in January organized a benevolent society, its object being to
help the poor and fallen among the Japanese women,
to give food and care to the sick, to provide a way for
children to be attended to while their mothers worked,
and to lead the wicked into the path of righteousness.
I put into this society all the money I had saved for
my future work, and secured over one hundred members for it. Shortly after the organizing of this society a poor Japanese woman who had been carrying

on an evil work died. As she had no relations in
this country the people among whom she lived took
care of her while she was sick, but they had no place
to bury her. Two men came to my office and wished
me to speak to my pastor about allowing them to
bury this woman in the Japanese Mission burial-
grounds. I did so, and told him that I thought this
a good opportunity to put into operation my plan of
doing benevolent work among these most degraded
and sunken people. He gladly granted their request,
and then they asked him to conduct the funeral service and invited me to accompany him. We went to
the undertaker's house, where the corpse was, and
where was gathered quite a company of men and
women. I looked carefully into their condition, and
when the service was over asked the manager to give
em time to speak. Standing up, I said : " I am very
glad to meet you, my dear country sisters. Will you
not all stand and look once more into the dead face of
this our sister ? What do you think about her face?
Is it not sorrowful and thin ? I can almost see her
sorrow-stricken heart when her life went out. Perhaps she had been homesick and wished to 'see her
parents and sisters and brothers, and died saying, ' I
hope to see once more my dear native place and my
mother and father.' Some ancient person has said,
' When a person dies his last words are good.' When
people are in good health, eat nice food, wear beautiful clothes, and are engaged in unclean business they

never remember their native land, but selfishly go on getting more and more and wanting still more and more. They never turn to see their own hearts covered up with wickedness, and do not prepare for death, although this is not our eternal home. When we die we must go back to the eternal home of our heavenly Father. This sister's mother, father, and relations are waiting for her and saying proudly to their friends every day: 'My daughter went to America, where she is getting a good education.' They do not know the sad condition in which she is; they never think of evil. Then, sisters, what do you think will happen when this sad message reaches her parents? The poor mother will perhaps die with a broken heart. Sisters, you have parents. Do not forget them, do not forget your loved native land. Pass not through the narrow and unclean streets, but walk in the right, large road." The women sobbed aloud and the men hung their heads. When I saw how they felt I said: "I trust that *you* are not engaged in wicked business, but if you find among your friends any one who does work that is not right please ask her to stop; and if you find those who are poor or in any trouble come and tell me, that I may help them. I have established a society for those who need help, and have a room all ready for them; therefore please come to me at any time." Then we went to the burial-ground, returning to the mission about eight o'clock in the evening. That night all my Japanese Christian friends met in the pastor's sitting-room, and he told them about what I had said. "Your words were very good," he said, turning to me. "Everybody has been afraid to speak against these wicked people, but you were not afraid."

It is the custom in Japan when a person has been dead seven days for the family to make a feast and invite all who attended the funeral. These people observed this custom, and invited me to the house of the chief man who had had charge of the woman's funeral. My friends feared to have me go; but I said I believed the people trusted me and would do me no harm, and accordingly went with the guide who was sent for me. On reaching the place I was seated in a pleasant room and served with a nice dinner. When through my dinner they asked me to speak, which I gladly did. At eleven o'clock I went back to the mission, accompanied by one of the men. Three women had asked to become members of my society, and some of the men had said: "I will stop gambling and drinking wine; therefore please put my name among your society members." About ten days after the chief man brought me five dollars. "We collected fifty-four dollars from among our company for the funeral," he said. "After expenses were paid ten dollars remained, and I wish to give half to the Japanese Mission and half to your society if you will please receive this small gift." I did so, and he went away with a glad heart.

Nearly every day I was visited by these people, many becoming members of the society and attending the Sunday services at the mission.

Thus was begun Christian work among fallen men and women. Every day I visited them, explained the Bible, and pleaded with them to do right. My friends begged me to stop, for they feared I would suffer harm; but I did not fear. I knew my God was always with me.

The work of the society is still carried on by Mrs. M. E. Harris, who is president. Many poor children are kept there, and when women and girls get out of work they stay there and take care of the children till they find a good place; then others come to take their place. Thus the work goes on, constantly changing and growing.

CHAPTER X.

A BACKSLIDER RECLAIMED.

ONE afternoon a Japanese young man came to my office and asked if I would listen to his story. On my answering that I would be pleased to do so he related the following: "I came to San Francisco one and a half years ago, accompanied by about twenty-five Japanese. One of the number had been a Christian many years, and he preached to us every day on the voyage. His preaching made us feel very happy; it comforted our hearts and made us forget our loneliness. Soon after we arrived here three of us believed on Christ, whom we had heard of during the voyage through this man's preaching, and we went to work to earn money for our education. Not long after we heard that our preacher had begun to drink and play cards. This made us feel very sad, and we begged him to stop, but he would not listen to our words. Then we determined on asking you to speak to him, and it is for that purpose that I come to you to-day." I said I feared he would not listen to me, as I was only a poor woman, but that I would try what I could do. That evening the young man accompanied me to the house of his friend and said to him, " Miss Sono wants to speak to you." " Well," he answered, his thick voice

and red face betokening the drunkard. He looked
intently at me for a long while, then remembered that
he had heard me speak at the poor woman's funeral.
I talked with him a long while, but apparently with
no good result, for he said, "Wine is a very good
thing. I love it very much. Indeed, I must love it,
because when I have trouble or am sad I can at once
become happy by taking the dear wine. It makes me
forget my poverty." I waited until he became more
sober, then asked him if his parents were living. He
said his mother, seventy years old, was living, and that
she had no other children. Then I said, the tears
running down my cheeks all the time I talked,
"Who is taking care of her now? It is your duty to
care for her. She has loved you very deeply, more
deeply than you can love her. You ought not to
come so far away while she is living. She is thinking of you every day, and waiting for you to return, for
she longs to see your face before she dies. She is old
and soon must die. Can you do her any good after
she dies?" His face was downcast while I talked;
then he said, "I thank you very much for your kindness to me. I will think seriously about what you
have said. It is very late now, and you had better go
back." When I reached the mission with my guide
it was almost twelve o'clock. From that time the
man began to attend regularly the Sunday meeting,
and during the week to talk with many of his friends.
The young man afterward thanked me for having

spoken to his friend and causing him to stop the use of wine. When I left San Francisco the reformed man met me at the station to say good-bye. My last words to him were, " Please do not forget your mother, but go back while she lives."

CHAPTER XI.

In May of 1889 my pastor advised me to attend the Chicago Training-School, of which Mrs. L. R. Meyer is principal. Accordingly, I made preparation to go, and on the eve of my leaving San Francisco was given a reception by my friends there.

After my departure Mrs. L. M. Carver, President of the Woman's Christian Temperance Union, of which I had become a member in April, kindly wrote an article to the *Union Signal*, descriptive of my work. Thinking it may be of interest, I insert it here:

"*June* 13, 1889.

" DEAR UNION SIGNAL: Truly it can be said of us that we are living in a time when to be living is sublime. Scarcely had the echoes of admiration and wonder, of fêting and parting for the lovely Ramabai died away, when, lo! as in a panoramic tableau, another Oriental scene is presented to our view, and Japan, the progressive island queen of the Orient, is to be honored and blessed with a native Christian woman reformer, Miss Cassie Tel Sono.

" Having been in comparative seclusion till near

the time of leaving our shores, we give a little of her history, which reads like a romance, and not only proves that 'truth is stranger than fiction,' but that 'His word shall not return unto him void, but shall accomplish that whereunto it is sent.' Belonging to the better class in her own country, her father being an *esha* (physician), and herself a *dai-gen* (lawyer), a thing unheard of for a woman in Japan, she was in a position to see the degraded and almost helpless condition of the women and children, especially of the lower classes.

"Catching glimpses through the missionary families of the favored lot of the wives and mothers of America, she determined to come to this country, learn the language, and become familiar with the customs of the people, then return to her native land and introduce a wide-spread reform.

"She landed in San Francisco in January, 1886, and found her first home in the Chinese and Japanese Mission of the Methodist Episcopal Church, the Rev. J. M. Masters being superintendent and pastor. Intent on the one idea of learning the language, she followed the advice of the Rev. Meyama, who was then on this coast, and went into an exemplary Christian family to assist in household duties and the care of children. Though wholly unused to any kind of manual labor, she succeeded by indomitable perseverance in making herself useful, and at the same time had in three months learned to read the First and

Second Readers quite satisfactorily, and had endeared herself to all.

"About this time the *gingko* (bank) in Japan, in which she had some money deposited for her future work of reform, having failed, she became greatly depressed, but, true to her heroic nature, she rose superior to all discouragements, and through the kindness of a noble Christian woman, Mrs. E. P. Keeney, who took her to her home and assisted her in every way, she was soon able to enter a young ladies' classical school, where she remained till she was graduated. In the meantime she had embraced Christianity, was baptized on Christmas day at her earnest request, and became a member of the Japanese Methodist Episcopal Church, of which the Rev. M. C. Harris, formerly missionary to Japan, is pastor.

"It was far from the purpose of Tel Sono to adopt the religion of this country. Her chief object was to avail herself of its educational and reformatory methods. But she soon learned that Christianity was what had placed America so far in advance of Japan.

"Now we see her trying to comprehend the great doctrine of justification by faith in a crucified and risen Saviour. Hitherto it had been her delight to argue with and confound the Japanese converts, which she could do so successfully that they avoided coming in contact with her sophistry. But, having once been convinced that Jesus was the only Saviour, she immediately set about trying to make amends for the past by becoming a missionary among her people, beginning her work of reform wherever she saw an opportunity of doing good. Having collected $100 for the relief of the needy and unfortunate among her countrymen, she established a benevolent society, which is already proving a great blessing to them.

"Last, but not least, she became interested in the Woman's Christian Temperance Union and united with the North San Francisco Union, Miss S. M. V. Cunimings president. Through her instrumentality and that of our co-worker, Rev. M. C. Harris, we expect to organize a Woman's Christian Temperance Union among the Japanese. A few days after adopting the white ribbon an incident occurred that is worthy of relating, as it shows how omnipotent is example and how helpful is the 'bit of white ribbon.'

"A lady who wished to do her honor invited her to a sumptuous farewell dinner; and, to tell it in her own language, she said : 'Every thing was very, very fine—soup and chickens, salad and cakes, and the little red wine-glasses to every plate. When they pour my wine I shake my head and say, "No, no, I drink no wine." The lady she say, "What you mean, Cassie ?" (her American name.) "You not like wine ?" Then I put my fingers on my white ribbon and say, "I belong to temperance society." Then all the glasses and wine go quick from the table.' This was told in a serio-comic manner that was laughable in the ex-

treme ; but a lump came up in our throat that would
not down, for we thought of the thousands in this
Christian land who were drinking wine to their ruin,
and how few there are who, like this noble Japanese
woman,

> " ' Dare to stand alone,
> Dare to have a purpose firm,
> Dare to make it known.'

"As she is now in Chicago to attend the school for
deaconesses preparatory to the great mission to
which she seems called of God, we trust these lines
may be instrumental in helping her to a better knowledge of our Christian temperance work.

" At a reception given her at the Japanese Mission
just before her departure, at which, among others, one
hundred Japanese students were present who vied in
doing her honor, she seized the opportunity to impress
them with the fact of the great evils from the use of
intoxicants and narcotics, and requested your corre-
spondent to speak to them of the dangers to which
they were exposed in this great city.

" Forgetful of self, her heart yearned over those
whom she was about to leave, and, speaking to them in
words of anxious tenderness, she made a deep and
lasting impression on their minds so receptive to good
influences.

" She will be missed by her people and by many
friends who have learned to love and esteem her for
her sterling Christian virtues, so indispensable to any

reformatory work. But we bid her God-speed on her
mission of love and mercy, and pray that she may be
spared to return to her native land to act a noble part
in rescuing the perishing millions of that lovely 'Sun-
rise Land.'"

I remained in Chicago until November, 1889, when
Mrs. Meyer sent me to the Missionary Training Insti-
tute in Brooklyn, N. Y., that I might have better ad-
vantages for studying the English branches. This
school, in which I am now studying, and of which
Mrs. L. D. Osborn is principal, is indeed a blessed and
pleasant home. I am perfectly satisfied here, and have
every opportunity of gaining a rich Christian experience. The light of God shines into the darkness of
my heart as I listen to Mrs. Osborn's good words of
counsel. All the students love me and show special
kindness to the stranger in their midst.

As there are no charges for board or tuition, I am
free from all financial embarrassment. Only those who
have known what it is to have a great work upon their
hearts and no means to prepare for the accomplishing of that work can know the joy of finding such a
haven as this.

My gratitude to my heavenly Father and to Mrs.
Osborn is unbounded. Never, never can I be un-
mindful of the love that has been shown me in this
school and the blessings I have received here.

My plan for the future is to establish a free

Christian school in my native place, where there are no Christians, no churches, no missionary schools. Already the voices from over the ocean are calling, "Come back quickly! Come and lead us into a better and a happier life."

I long to return that I may live and work and die for my heathen sisters. God has led me to America, he has blessed me with his own salvation, has provided for the needs of my body and soul; and now he bids me go back to the home-land and there make known his law.

Christian sisters, you can promote the accomplishing of my purpose. Those whom I seek to help, those who are being held in slavery and ignorance, and whom I long to liberate, are your sisters too, for God "hath made of one blood all nations of men." When you come up before the judgment-throne and meet those throngs for whom I plead, your reward will be the greater if among them there are those whom you have helped to save; and the less if there are those whom you might have helped to save but did not, and who, therefore, must hear the awful word, "Depart!"

Do to-day what you will wish you had done when time with its opportunities is past. For Jesus' sake, withhold not your prayers, your sympathy, your aid!

THE END.